Keena Ford

AND THE SECOND-GRADE
★ MIX-UP ★

Keena Ford

AND THE SECOND-GRADE
★ MIX-UP ★

MELISSA THOMSON

pictures by
FRANK MORRISON

DIAL BOOKS
FOR YOUNG READERS

DIAL BOOKS FOR YOUNG READERS
A division of Penguin Young Readers Group
Published by The Penguin Group
Penguin Group (USA) Inc., 375 Hudson Street, New York, NY 10014, U.S.A.
Penguin Group (Canada), 90 Eglinton Avenue East, Suite 700, Toronto, Ontario,
Canada M4P 2Y3 (a division of Pearson Penguin Canada Inc.)
Penguin Books Ltd, 80 Strand, London WC2R 0RL, England
Penguin Ireland, 25 St. Stephen's Green, Dublin 2, Ireland
(a division of Penguin Books Ltd)
Penguin Group (Australia), 250 Camberwell Road,
Camberwell, Victoria 3124, Australia
(a division of Pearson Australia Group Pty Ltd)
Penguin Books India Pvt Ltd, 11 Community Centre,
Panchsheel Park, New Delhi - 110 017, India
Penguin Group (NZ), 67 Apollo Drive, Rosedale, North Shore 0632, New Zealand
(a division of Pearson New Zealand Ltd)
Penguin Books (South Africa) (Pty) Ltd, 24 Sturdee Avenue,
Rosebank, Johannesburg 2196, South Africa
Penguin Books Ltd, Registered Offices:
80 Strand, London WC2R 0RL, England

Designed by Jasmin Rubero
Text set in Cochin medium
Printed in the U.S.A.

5 7 9 10 8 6 4

Library of Congress Cataloging-in-Publication Data
Thomson, Melissa, date.
Keena Ford and the second-grade mix-up / by Melissa Thomson ;
pictures by Frank Morrison.
p. cm.
Summary: Keena Ford chronicles her many mishaps as she begins second grade.
ISBN: 978-0-8037-3263-6
[1. Schools—Fiction. 2. African Americans—Fiction. 3.
Diaries—Fiction.] I. Morrison, Frank, date, ill. II. Title.
PZ7.T37195Ke 2008
[Fic]—dc22
2007043749

To the students of Emery Elementary
in Washington, DC
—M.T.

To my wonderful daughter Nia
—F.M.

WEDNESDAY, AUGUST 25
4:30 P.M.

I'm Keena, and I am the MOST important person in this journal, because it is MY journal. But there are some other important people too, like my mom and my brother, Brian. I live with them in our apartment in Washington, DC. Brian is starting middle school and he thinks he is SO cool. But he still sleeps with his blankie! Ha! I haven't told his friends yet. I'm waiting for the perfect time.

My dad is really important too. He lives in Maryland and I visit him on weekends. He has a bald head and a fish named Henry.

Someone else who is important is my very best friend, Eric. He and his dad live in our building in the apartment right above ours. This other girl in our building, Tiffany Harris, says I can't be best friends with a boy, but what does she know? I tried being friends with her, but all we did was have stupid tea parties. And her tea tasted like a wet paper bag.

I guess I should write down that Mr. Lemon is important too. He teaches time-out. It's the class where you go if you broke a rule by mistake. You go there when the other kids go outside to play after lunch. Mr. Lemon and I spend a LOT of time together.

I think I will probably write about some other people, but they won't be as important as the ones I already said.

My mom got me this journal because I behaved myself at the doctor's office this afternoon. It was my back-to-school checkup, and I had to get one shot. I cried, but I didn't pinch anyone. At the doctor's office, the nurse is allowed to stick you with needles, but you are not allowed to pinch. I learned this last year when I had to get a shot. The nurse said, "This will feel like a pinch for just a second." And then I said, "YOW!!" because it hurt, and hurt for a LONG time. Then I said, "That did NOT pinch for just a second. It pinched for a very long time." She just looked at me, so I showed her what I was talking about. I grabbed her arm and pinched—HARD. Just so she would know what it really felt like, instead of telling kids it will only pinch for a second. Then I learned that you never, ever pinch or you get in big trouble. Last year I did NOT get a journal.

But this year I was very good, so Mom let me pick out my journal myself. She said writing in a journal is a great idea because I can get my feelings out without yelling or pinching. And I can write down the things that you are not supposed to say out loud, like: "Brian just passed gas."

I say a lot of things that you are not supposed to say out loud. I think I will have a lot to write in my new journal.

I am a very good writer for my age. My teacher last year told me that. She also said that if I spent more time writing and less time worrying about other people's business, then I could be a famous

writer someday. But if I don't pay attention to other people's business, what will
I write about?

Mom bought me a dictionary to go
with my journal so I can spell big words.
Already I had to look up "attention,"
"worrying," and "business." But I didn't
have to look up "dictionary" because it's
right on the front of the dictionary. Isn't
that handy?

THURSDAY, AUGUST 26
4:00 P.M.

Look! So far I have been writing in my journal every day. I knew I would have a lot to write about. Today was a big day because it was the last morning of camp for Eric and me. Last night Eric called me and sounded very mysterious. He said, "Be sure to wear your camp T-shirt tomorrow."

"But MONDAYS are camp T-shirt days," I said. "Tomorrow is Wacky Thursday." I had already picked out my final Wacky Thursday outfit. I was going to wear what I wore for Halloween last year when I was a cat who was also a princess and also a witch.

"Just please wear your T-shirt, Keena. I will explain the plan tomorrow," Eric said.

"Or you could explain it right now," I said.

"What's that? Keena? I can't hear you. I think we are going through a tunnel." Then I heard a clicking sound as he hung up the phone. I know that sometimes when people drive through tunnels their phones stop working. But there is no tunnel in Eric's apartment, unless you count the time we tried to dig a tunnel to my apartment through a loose floor tile. We got in big trouble for that one.

I thought about not wearing my T-shirt to show Eric he's not the boss of me, but I was too curious to see what he had planned. So when Eric arrived this morning, I was wearing my T-shirt and my cat ears. I opened the door to see Eric in his T-shirt, hiding something behind his back.

"Ta-daaaa!" he said, and held out two permanent markers.

"Huh?" I said.

"When we get to camp, we'll get everyone to sign our T-shirts with a permanent marker. Then we will always remember our friends from camp!" Eric seemed very excited.

I tried to act excited too, because even if Eric's great ideas aren't that great, he IS my very best friend.

"Okay," I said. I was thinking to myself, "What's so great about two old markers?" But at least I had my cat ears.

You know what, though? Eric's idea was really good! We got all of the other kids and even the counselors to sign our T-shirts. Everyone else wished they had worn their camp T-shirts too. It was lots of fun with only one problem. The problem was that the ink went through the shirt and onto my skin in some places, so it says "Nancy" on my arm and "Leonda" on my stomach. I can't quite seem to wash it off. But I'm sure my mom can fix it with a little scrubbing, once I show her.

7:00 P.M.

Every day after camp Eric and I have been working on our playhouse. Well, it's not really a playhouse. We call it a Homework Hut. It's a place for us to sit and work on our homework once we are in second grade. Second grade has lots of homework, so Eric and I need a pretty quiet place to work on all of it. And since we know for sure that we will be in the same class, it makes sense for us to work together. We have a big box from Mom's new refrigerator. Eric got two old pillows that will be our seats. I have been painting the Homework Hut. We keep it on the balcony behind my apartment, and we cover it with plastic bags every night. It looks really, really cool. It is going to be so fun to do our homework in the Homework Hut. I think second grade is going to be the best year ever.

FRIDAY, AUGUST 27
8:00 P.M.

Today was the worst day EVER. Last night I forgot to put the cover on the Homework Hut. Mom called me to set the table when I was about to cover the hut. I knew she had made a pudding pie, and that is my very favorite dessert. So I didn't want to make her mad by not setting the table right away. Then she might say, "No pudding pie for you, Keena Ford!"

So I got my pudding pie, but I ruined the Homework Hut. We had a thunderstorm and the whole thing is wet. It's bad. Really bad. The paint dripped all down the side, and now it looks like it says "HORK HU." But that is not even the most awful thing that happened today! Here is the MOST awful thing:

Eric and I are not going to be in the same class.

I got a letter from school today. From the SCHOOL PRINCIPAL. At first I was afraid that maybe she had found out that I was the one who got the jump rope stuck in Mr. Lemon's DVD player by mistake.

But the letter wasn't about Mr. Lemon's DVD player. It was about Eric and me NOT BEING IN THE SAME CLASS for sure. Know why? Because Eric is a boy and I am a girl. That's right. Our principal is putting boys and girls in different classes.

I hope this doesn't mean my classroom will have a lot of pink.

Now there's no reason to even fix up the Homework Hut.

SATURDAY, AUGUST 28
8:30 A.M.

I am watching cartoons with Brian while we are waiting for Dad to pick us up to go to Maryland. We watch two cartoons every Saturday morning. The first cartoon is about machines that fight for no reason, and the second cartoon is about funny animals on a farm. When

you have to watch one stupid cartoon before you get to watch a good cartoon it is called a compromise.

6:30 P.M.

I am at Dad's house. Brian is playing with his friend Maryland Jason. I call him Maryland Jason because Brian has another friend named Jason in DC. Brian says not to say "Maryland Jason," because it sounds dumb, and he also says not to call it "playing," because once you are older you just call it "hanging out."

Since Brian went to Maryland Jason's,

that means I got to talk to Dad alone. When I told him I was going to be in a class with a bunch of girls he just smiled at me like it was funny. And I said, "It's NOT funny! How would you like to be covered in pink and drinking paper-bag tea every day?" Then he looked at me like I was a little bit crazy. And he said maybe we should go out for coffee and talk about it.

Going out for coffee with Dad is pretty much my favorite thing ever. For one thing, I get to order for myself. I always order a "decaf with skim milk, hold the coffee." When you say "hold" something, it means "Do NOT put that on my food."

Like if you think spinach is nasty, you say, "Hold the spinach." And then you don't get nasty spinach on your plate. This only works when you go out to eat, though. It doesn't work on moms or dads. They will never, ever hold the spinach.

Anyway, I know that when I order a "decaf with skim milk, hold the coffee," that means I'm not really drinking coffee. I am just drinking milk. But the coffee shop smells like coffee, and I get to drink out of a coffee mug. So I feel like a real grown-up.

Dad and I like to have grown-up talks at the coffee shop. Sometimes we talk about how it can be a little bit hard for me to live in two different places. Sometimes we talk about how I will try to stay out of trouble so my teacher stops calling my dad's cell phone and using up his daytime minutes.

Today we were talking about how SUPER-SAD I was that Eric and I weren't going to be in the same class. And how I was going to be in a class with all girls. Not that I have a problem with girls—after all, I am a girl, right?—but I don't like to wear skirts very much. Or play with dolls. I used to play with them sometimes, you know, when I was really bored, but Brian would make fun of me. So now when I am really bored I just play tic-tac-toe against myself.

There is another teeny-tiny reason why I don't want to be in a class with all girls. If all of the second-grade girls are in one class, it means that Linny Berry will be in my class for sure. And we don't exactly get along. I think it started when I might have taken her green crayon. Linny got mad, and she didn't invite me to her birthday party. It was on a Saturday, and she invited all the other girls in our first-grade class. So on Monday they all came to school wearing these necklaces they got at Linny's birthday party. And I felt really bad that I didn't have one.

So I called her a bad, awful, horrible name. I called her the bad name three times in a row. That's how mad I was about that stupid necklace. And Linny started to cry. The teacher called my mom but she was in a meeting, so then the teacher called my dad and used up some more of his daytime minutes. Linny whispered that she hated me, but the teacher didn't hear. Then I got sent to Mr. Lemon, the time-out teacher, and we had that little mix-up with the jump rope.

And that is why I can't be in the same class as Linny Berry.

While I was thinking about Linny

Berry, Dad asked, "Remember when you and Eric didn't speak for three days last year?"

I said I remembered. We got in a great big fight because . . . well, I can't remember why. I remember being really mad, though. "I can't remember why we were fighting," I admitted.

"It was probably because you were spending too much time together," Dad said. "Sometimes if you spend all of your time with one person, you start to fight about silly things. So maybe if you and Eric are in different classes, you'll be even better friends."

"Kind of like how you and Mom don't

yell at each other now that you live in Maryland?" I asked.

Dad gave a tiny nod. Then he smiled, but he looked a little bit sad too. Then he said we should probably go home. So I drank the rest of my milk really fast. And I wiped off my milk mustache without having to be told.

MONDAY, AUGUST 30
9:00 P.M.

Tomorrow is the first day of school!
Mom, Brian, and I went shopping
today. I had to get new uniforms. Our
school uniform is green pants or a green
skirt with a white button-down shirt.
The good thing about uniforms is that
you can get an award for wearing your

uniform every day, even if you don't get any other awards like "Good Citizen" or "Most Improved." I also got a cool belt that sparkles. And I got TWO pairs of shoes! Brian and Mom got in a fight because he wanted shoes that cost one hundred dollars. Mom said, "Forget it."

I said, "I am not complaining about my new things, Mommy. I am just so happy to be shopping with you." And I gave her a big smile. She said, "Well, at least someone is grateful for their new clothes." Then Brian called me a mean name.

I got so excited about my new belt and shoes that I almost forgot about Linny Berry and my all-girl class. Almost.

It is taking me a long time to fall asleep. I started thinking again about how I was not going to be in the same class as Eric. I have decided that I will probably hate second grade.

TUESDAY, AUGUST 31
10:30 A.M.

I LOVE second grade!!!!!!

There's some pink in our classroom, but there are other colors too. Our classroom looks really cool. We have four computers where we can play math and reading games. We have beanbag chairs where we can sit and read books. The beanbags are my second-favorite thing about my new class because I need a soft place to sit when I read. Reading at my desk makes my elbows hurt.

My first-favorite thing about second grade is my TEACHER. Her name is Ms. Campbell, and she is wearing a blue shirt and a COOL BELT WITH SPAR-KLES. Just like mine!! She let us pick our own seats. I sat far, far away from Linny Berry. And Ms. Campbell didn't read us a long list of boring rules. She said WE get to write the rules for our classroom!

Ms. Campbell is so cool.

This morning she told us that every

morning after we read together, we are going to sit down quietly and write in our journals. Then she gave each of us a notebook that said "Journal" on the cover.

I raised my hand.

"Yes, Keena?" Ms. Campbell said.

"Ummm . . . this is a very nice journal you have given me, Ms. Campbell, but I already have a journal," I told her. "Can I write in that one instead?"

I pressed my lips together and waited for her to say that it wouldn't be fair for me to use a different journal than everyone else. But she didn't! She said . . .

"Sure, Keena, that would be fine."

I LOVE second grade!!

7:30 P.M.

Eric came over after school today, and we talked about our new classes. Actually, I did most of the talking. I told him about how Ms. Campbell is going to let us make the rules and how she let me use my very own journal even though it wasn't like the journals that the other girls had. I told him about everything we did. Then I asked, "How was the boy class?"

Eric looked like he was thinking for a minute. I let him do his thinking. I didn't say, "Hello!!! I asked you a question!"

because Mr. Lemon said that is a rude thing to say. Then Eric said, "My class was really fun too. It was as fun as your class. Maybe even more fun. Ms. Hanson lets us chew gum in class. And she said we can do all of our work with a pen."

"You get to write with a PEN?!" I shouted. "I thought it was against the law to write with a pen in the second grade." I only write with a pen when I do art projects at home. Or when I have to write apology letters at home. Eric must be very excited.

But Eric didn't look very excited. He was looking at the floor beside my left shoe. Then he said he had to go home.

WEDNESDAY, SEPTEMBER 1
10:30 A.M.

This morning we wrote our names and birthdays on paper birthday cakes. Then we got to color the birthday cakes using any color we wanted.

My birthday is February 9. My mom calls me her valentine because I was born very close to Valentine's Day. But I didn't write my birthday as February 9. I wrote it a special way with just numbers that I learned from Brian. You write a number for the day and a number for the month. And you put a line between the numbers. The day of my birthday is 9, and the month is 2, because February is the second month of the year. So I wrote: 9/2.

I am lucky to have an older brother who teaches me things.

Now we are writing in our journals and Ms. Campbell is hanging up our birthday cakes. She has the names of the months hanging on the walls. She is putting our cakes next to the name of the month of our birthday.

Wait . . . she just taped my cake next to "September."

Uh-oh.

And just now she said, "Excuse me, ladies. I am very excited to report that we have a class birthday tomorrow, September 2. Keena Ford will be the first student to wear our special birthday crown." Then she looked at me and smiled. "Keena, I hope you like chocolate cake," she said.

I tried to open my mouth to tell Ms. Campbell that there must be some mistake. My birthday is February 9. But I thought about that birthday crown. And I thought about the cake. I love birthday cake almost as much as I love pudding

pie. So when I opened my mouth, this was what came out:

"Yes, Ms. Campbell. I LOVE choco-late cake."

8:30 P.M.

When Brian came home from school, I wrote down 9/2 and showed it to him. I said, "You told me this says February 9."

"That says September 2," he said.

"No," I told him. "My birthday is on the ninth, and February is the second month of the year."

"I know THAT, smarty-pants," Brian said. "But in America, you write the

MONTH first. Then the day. It should look like this . . . "

Then he took my pencil and paper and wrote 2/9.

I looked at his 2/9. Then I looked at my 9/2. Then I understood my big, big mistake.

I think I have gotten myself into some kind of a mess.

"Why are you asking me these dumb questions, anyway?" Brian wanted to know.

I told him it was for my homework. Then I ran to my room really fast. I needed to think of a plan to get myself out of trouble.

I thought about my big mistake for one hour. Ms. Campbell thinks my birthday is tomorrow, but it's not until February. I didn't mean to lie to Ms. Campbell. If I let her keep thinking that my birthday is tomorrow, that is kind of a lie. All I have to do is tell Ms. Campbell about the mix-up. I will explain that my birthday is NOT September 2. And if she asks why I didn't tell her before she made a chocolate cake, then I can just tell her that I got confused. I thought about this plan to tell her the truth. Then I came up with another plan: I will just pretend to be sick tomorrow.

THURSDAY, SEPTEMBER 2
10:30 A.M.

Last night I coughed a little bit when Mom tucked me in. Just so she might think I was coming down with something. Then this morning when she woke me up I coughed REALLY, REALLY loud.

Mom pretended she didn't hear me.

When she turned the lights on, I said,

"Could you turn those off? My head is pounding."

She said that my breakfast was ready.

I guess she wasn't getting the hint that I was trying to be sick. So I said, "I feel just plain awful. I think I have the flu. I can't go to school today."

I waited for Mom to say, "I'm sorry, Valentine. Where does it hurt? I'll make you some chicken soup." But she didn't. Instead she said, "Keena, I don't have time for you to be sick all week. If you're really sick, I will take you to the doctor for some shots. Then you will feel better right away. It's probably nothing a few needles can't fix." She looked like she really meant it about the needles.

Lying to a teacher is really bad. But getting stuck with needles when I wasn't sick seemed even worse. I got up and put my school clothes on right away. I decided to think of a new plan.

When Mom was walking me to school she kept looking at me kind of funny. I think my eyes were very big and round because I was thinking so hard about my new plan. When she gave me a kiss at the door to school she looked at me for a second. Then she said, "Keena, if you start to feel worse, have the school call me. I will take you to the doctor." Then she looked

at me funny again. I just nodded with my eyes still big and round. I wanted to shout, "Help! It's not my birthday!" but I just said, "Okay. Bye, Mommy."

My new plan was going to be the same as my first plan: to tell Ms. Campbell the truth. But when I got to my classroom Ms. Campbell had the birthday crown sitting on my desk. It was purple with silver sparkles and it said "BIRTHDAY GIRL" in big silver letters.

It was so cool.

I put the birthday crown on my head.

On one side of the chalkboard, Ms. Campbell had written with different-colored chalk: "Happy birthday, Keena

Ford!" She had drawn three balloons. It was the first time I had gotten my name on the board and it didn't mean that I was in big trouble.

I knew I needed to tell Ms. Campbell that today wasn't really my birthday. So I raised my hand. I could feel my heart beating really fast. She said, "Yes, Keena?" and looked at me with a big smile on her face. She was smiling at me because it was my special day. And all I said was, "I like the balloons on the board, Ms. Campbell." And even though I DID like the balloons on the board, I felt like a big fat liar.

Now I'm sitting here with this birthday crown on my head, trying to think of what to tell Ms. Campbell. I have to tell her the truth before lunch. After lunch I will see Eric, and he will know it's not my birthday. And he will tell my class. Then I'll be in trouble.

3:30 P.M.

I meant to tell Ms. Campbell when we were lining up for lunch. I had taken off my birthday crown and set it on my desk. When Ms. Campbell said, "Keena, are you not going to wear your birthday crown to lunch?" that was when I was going to say:

"No, Ms. Campbell, I am not going to wear my crown to lunch because it is not really my birthday. My birthday is February 9."

But I didn't say that. I didn't say it because right before Ms. Campbell asked about the crown, she had gotten something out of the little refrigerator right behind her desk, and she had shown it to me. It was a chocolate cake that said "Happy birthday, Keena!" in light purple frosting.

That cake looked DELICIOUS. I really, really wanted a piece of that cake.

So I told Ms. Campbell that I wasn't

wearing the crown because I didn't want it to get dirty at recess.

It was true that I DIDN'T want the crown to get dirty. But I still felt like a big fat liar.

When we got to lunch, I looked over at the table where Ms. Hanson's class was sitting. I was looking for Eric. I knew that if he heard something about the chocolate cake, then everyone would find out it wasn't my birthday. I didn't see Eric at the table. I guessed he was in the bathroom.

Then I remembered—Eric had to go to the dentist! He was mad about going because he would miss lunch and recess but he would have to come back for math. I decided there was no way that Eric would be back before the end of recess. I also decided no one would know if I was celebrating my birthday a little early. So I raised my hand. "Ms. Campbell, can I go get the birthday crown? I think I want to wear it after all."

After recess Ms. Campbell announced that we were having a special treat. I knew it was my birthday cake. She called everyone over to the carpet near her desk. All of the other girls had to sit, but I got to stand near the cake. Ms. Campbell and the class started singing "Happy Birthday" to ME. Even Linny

Berry was singing. It was so exciting. I started to kind of believe that it really WAS my birthday. I had a big smile on my face. I even sang at the end of the song, except instead of singing "Happy birthday, dear Keena," I sang "Happy birthday, dear me." I squeezed my eyes shut and opened my mouth really wide. I felt like I was on stage. I sang the last line as loud as I could: "HAPPY BIRTHDAY TO MEEEE!"

All of a sudden I realized that I had been singing the end of the song all by myself. Everyone else had stopped singing. I opened my eyes. Ms. Campbell and my classmates were looking toward the door. I thought maybe there was another surprise, like balloons or a pony, so I looked too.

There were no balloons in the doorway. There wasn't a pony there either.

Instead, standing in the doorway was . . . my mom.

Boy, was I ever surprised.

My mom looked surprised too.

Ms. Campbell said, "Hello, Ms. Ford. Did you come to celebrate Keena's birthday?"

My mom stood with her mouth open for a few seconds. She looked at me. I could feel my face getting warm. Then she said to Ms. Campbell, "No, I came to see if Keena was feeling better. She said she felt sick this morning, and I didn't let her stay home. I wanted to see if she was okay. It looks like she is just fine." She looked at me with her eyebrows raised. When my mom raises her eyebrows, it means I have some explaining to do.

Ms. Campbell said, "Oh no! Sick on her birthday? I didn't know. She didn't say anything to me."

Then my mom said, "May I speak to Keena in the hallway, please?"

It took me a long time to walk from Ms. Campbell's desk to the classroom door. When I got to the door, my mom took my hand and pulled me into the hallway. Then she took the birthday crown off my head.

She leaned down really close to my face. "Keena," she said in a loud whisper, "what is going on?" She did not look happy. My face got very, very warm.

"M-Ms. Campbell thinks today is my birthday," I said.

"I noticed that," my mom said. "I want you to tell me RIGHT NOW why Ms. Campbell thinks today is your birthday." Her voice was a little louder this time. And she looked really, really mad.

"I wrote the date wrong on my paper cake," I said. I told her how I wrote

9/2 instead of 2/9, so Ms. Campbell thought my birthday was September 2. I thought Mom might feel sorry for me because I got so confused.

She did not.

She said, "Keena, when did you first know that Ms. Campbell thought your birthday was today?"

"Yesterday," I admitted.

"Why did you not tell her right away that your birthday is in February?" she asked.

I didn't answer for a little while. Then I whispered, "Because of the chocolate cake."

Mom stared at me. Then she said,

"Keena, your teacher spent time making you a birthday cake when it wasn't your birthday. Maybe you didn't lie on purpose, but you didn't tell the truth either. I am very disappointed in you." She frowned at me. Then she said something that was even worse than being disappointed. She said, "I want you to go back in that classroom right now and tell your teacher and classmates the truth."

"Yes, ma'am," I whispered. Then I stood still for a long time.

"NOW, Keena," she said.

When we walked back into the room, all of the other girls were sitting at their desks eating cake. "Your cake is on your desk, Keena," Ms. Campbell said. "And we saved a piece for you, Ms. Ford," she told my mom.

"Thank you, Ms. Campbell, but Keena has something she needs to tell you and the class," my mom said. "Go ahead, Keena."

I looked at the floor. "My birthday is February 9," I whispered.

"Speak up, Keena," my mom said sternly.

I closed my eyes tightly. "My birthday," I said louder, "is February 9."

I opened my eyes and looked at Ms. Campbell. She looked at me and then at Mom. "I'm afraid I don't under-stand," she said.

"Keena wrote her birthday back-wards," Mom explained. "So you thought her birthday was today. Then she did not tell you the truth. I am very disap-pointed in her behavior. And I am sorry that you went to all that trouble to make a cake." Then Mom turned and looked at me. "Keena," she said, "I am going to have to think about your punishment. I will see you at home." Then she left the classroom.

I stood in the front of the room alone. I felt very, very small.

Ms. Campbell took the piece of cake

off my desk. She looked very serious. "Keena, I know this started as a numbers mistake. But you should have told me the truth. So you do not get to eat any cake. And you know what else?"

I waited for her to send me to Mr. Lemon's time-out classroom. But she didn't. She said, "I think we need a lesson in how to write the date using numbers. Take your seat, Keena."

Then Ms. Campbell showed us how to use numbers to write the date. Even though I will never, ever forget how to write the date using numbers, I think I'll stick to writing out the name of the month from now on.

When I got home, Mom said, "Keena, I have decided that you will not be allowed to watch TV or have dessert for one week. I also want you to go to your room right after dinner and think about what you did wrong." I nodded. "Also," she said, "I bought you a bottle of ginger ale when I thought you were sick. But you lied to me about being sick, so I am going to give your ginger ale to Brian." I nodded again, but I felt sad. Ginger ale is my favorite drink. I also felt sad because I knew Brian would make fun of me when he heard about my big fat lie.

Brian just came into my room. He was holding the ginger ale bottle. "Mom told me about your fake birthday," he said. "That was really dumb, Keena."

"I know," I said.

"I was wondering why you were asking me all those questions." Brian was smiling like he was about to laugh at me.

I felt my face get warm again.

Then Brian said, "Sorry you got so confused." He set the ginger ale bottle on my bedside table. "You can have that if you want," he said. Then he started walking out of the room. "Don't tell Mom," he said over his shoulder.

"Thanks, Brian," I said. But I don't think he heard me.

So I got a piece of white paper and some crayons out of my art box. I drew a tall boy wearing shorts and a T-shirt. "BEST BROTHER!" I wrote in big letters. Even though I wasn't supposed to leave my room, I tiptoed into the hallway. Brian's door was closed. I slid the paper under his door and ran back to my room. I looked at the ginger ale. It felt like a birthday present. I put the bottle in a drawer and jumped into bed.

FRIDAY, SEPTEMBER 3
10:30 A.M.

This morning I didn't want to go to school.
I thought Ms. Campbell hated me for
sure. But when I got to the classroom,
she just smiled and said, "Good morning,
Keena," like I was not a big fat liar. So
I felt better.

While Ms. Campbell was still in the

hall saying good morning to the students, Tiffany Harris came into the room. "You don't even know your own birthday," she said in a very mean voice. "Are you going to say today is your birthday too?" Then she stuck her tongue out at me.

I was about to call her a mean name, when Linny Berry said, "It's not nice to tease someone who made a mistake. So just close your mouth, Tiffany." I looked at Linny. "Thank you," I said. But she looked away. I guess she still hates me. Maybe she just hates Tiffany even more.

After all of the girls were sitting at their desks, Ms. Campbell said, "I think today is a good day to make the list of rules for our classroom. You are going to work with a partner to come up with some ideas for class rules. Then you will share your list with the class." Guess who she said had to be my partner?

Linny Berry.

Linny moved her chair near my desk. And we both looked at our knees for about one minute. Then I looked at Linny. I said in my quiet voice, "Maybe we should make a rule that you should not take someone's green crayon. Even if you didn't mean to."

Linny said, "That is a good rule, Keena."

Then she said, "I'm sorry I didn't invite you to my birthday party."

I said, "I'm sorry I called you a very bad name. Three times."

Then Linny said maybe we should make a rule that you shouldn't call anyone a very bad name. I told her that was a good rule. And Ms. Campbell thought we had good rules too! Although she didn't understand about the green crayon. She said we shouldn't take someone else's crayon of any color. Linny smiled at me when she said that. I think we are going to be friends! I think Friday is my lucky day!

1:30 P.M.

Friday is the most terrible day in the whole wide world. I am in time-out with Mr. Lemon.

4:30 P.M.

Here's what happened: When we went outside to play after lunch, Ms. Hanson was outside with the boy class. I saw Eric waiting for me at the monkey bars. That is our favorite place to play. But then Linny Berry said, "Hey, do you want to play on the slide?" I decided I

should probably play with Linny so she would be my friend for sure. So I said yes. Linny and I started taking turns on the slide. We were sliding pretty fast. Then Linny said, "Hey! Watch this!" She went down the slide headfirst. I was about to go down the slide headfirst too, when I heard Ms. Campbell say, "Linny Berry! That is not safe. Please have a seat." I decided that going down the slide head-first wasn't such a good idea if it meant I would have to sit down. So I went over to the monkey bars and started talking to Eric. I told him that Linny Berry and I were going to be friends! I told him all about our class rules and how Linny said she was sorry that she didn't invite me to her birthday party. I thought Eric would be very excited.

But Eric didn't look excited. He said, "Oh yeah? Well Ms. Hanson said that we don't have to follow ANY rules. And she said that she made a pudding pie for us. She said that she is going to make a pudding pie for us every day."

I was so amazed. Pudding pie? Every day?

"I wish I could be in your class when you eat pudding pie," I said to Eric.

"Well, too bad for you," he said in kind of a mean way. But I didn't say anything back. I could only think about

that pudding pie. When I eat pudding pie, I like to drink milk. The last time my mom made pudding pie, I drank three glasses of milk.

Thinking about all of that milk made me have to go to the bathroom REALLY bad.

So I asked Ms. Campbell if I could go inside and go to the bathroom. I waited for her to say, "No, Keena, we will stop at the bathroom on our way back to class." But she didn't. She said . . .

"Sure, Keena, that would be fine."

So I went to the bathroom. After I went to the bathroom I think I was supposed to go right back outside. But I didn't. I went into Ms. Hanson's class-room. I was walking by her door when I noticed that there was a very sharp pencil on every desk. Why did they have pencils? They were supposed to write in pen. So I walked into the class-room to look for the pens. I didn't see pens anywhere. I DID see a big, long list of rules taped to the wall.

Just then I heard the bell ring. I knew I should run back outside. Or at least GET OUT of Ms. Hanson's classroom. But I didn't. I needed to look for one more thing.

I needed to look for pudding pie.

I looked on the table at the front of

the room. There was no pudding pie. I didn't see pudding pie on the bookshelf. So I walked to the back of the room where Ms. Hanson's desk faced the door. That's when I heard a lot of feet outside the door. Ms. Hanson's class was back!

And that's when I crawled under Ms. Hanson's desk.

I folded my knees up near my shoulders and tried to breathe very, very quietly. I could hear my heart beating loud and heavy like a stomping foot. Then I heard people coming into the classroom.

Ms. Hanson said, "Frederick, do NOT come into this classroom chewing gum."

Rules, pencils, and NO gum? Right then I knew there was no pudding pie. Eric must have made up ALL of that stuff! Why would he do that?!

I heard chairs scraping against the floor as the boys sat down. I started to plan my escape. Maybe they would go to the bathroom, and I could run back into the girls' bathroom. Then I could tell Ms. Campbell that I had been feeling sick. It seemed like a good plan.

Ms. Hanson said, "Remember that you are now going to read silently for ten minutes. ABSOLUTELY NO TALK-ING."

Ten minutes?!?! Maybe they would

go to the bathroom after that. I heard Ms. Hanson's shoes clicking on the floor. The clicking was getting louder. I thought about all of the movies I had seen where a person is hiding. The person looking for them walks right by but doesn't spot them. And then everyone thinks, "Whew, that was close."

But this wasn't a movie. The clicking was getting even louder. Ms. Hanson's desk chair started to move. Then she sat in it. I could see her knees and the bottom part of her legs. Her legs were crossed. One foot was on the floor, and the other foot was swinging back and forth slowly. Every time she would swing her foot, it would get a little bit closer to my face.

And then Ms. Hanson kicked me. Right in the side of the head. I said, "Yowp!" and Ms. Hanson said, "What?!" Then she pushed her chair away from her desk and saw me. And she said, "EEEEE!"

I think I startled her. But she got over it pretty fast. The next thing she said was, "WHO ARE YOU AND WHAT ARE YOU DOING UNDER MY DESK?"

I scrambled out from under that desk as fast as I could. I stood up. Then I tried to say, "I'm Keena Ford," but I couldn't say anything. I could feel my face getting

very, very warm. And my eyes started to get a little bit wet. And my lip started to wobble.

I heard a boy's voice say loudly, "That's Keena. She is in Ms. Campbell's class."

I knew the voice was Eric's. Ms. Hanson looked at Eric. Then she looked back at me. She said, "Eric, go get Ms. Campbell."

Ms. Campbell must have been in the hallway at the water fountain, because she came into Ms. Hanson's room in about three seconds. My whole class must have been in the hallway too, because they all crowded in the doorway of Ms. Hanson's room.

"Ms. Campbell," Ms. Hanson said, "I have just found one of your students under my desk."

Ms. Campbell looked at me. She opened her mouth wide, like she was at the dentist. I think it was from surprise. Then she said, "Keena Ford! What on EARTH were you doing under Ms. Hanson's desk?" She moved her eyebrows close together to make an angry face, but her lips were pressed together like she was trying not to smile.

Even though Ms. Campbell didn't look that mad, I still couldn't talk.

I heard Eric's voice again. He sounded much quieter this time. "I know what

Keena was doing," he said. "She wanted to see our class because she thought it was maybe more fun than her class. Because I told her that it was. She said she wished she could be in our class."

I looked back at Ms. Campbell. Now she definitely wasn't smiling. Her face looked like it had fallen down a little bit. Her shoulders dropped down too. She looked just like Brian when he didn't make the basketball team. She looked sad and disappointed.

I wanted to tell Ms. Campbell that I thought she was the greatest teacher ever. I wanted to tell her our class was the MOST fun. But my lip started to wobble even more, and the tears started falling down my face. I couldn't say anything at all.

Ms. Campbell sent me to Mr. Lemon right away. She sent a very long note with me. It was much longer than the notes I got last year. Those always said, "Keena to Mr. Lemon's room—NOT following directions!!"

Mr. Lemon read every single word of the long note. Then he looked at me. "Well, Miss Ford," he said, "I suppose you must first write an apology to Ms. Hanson."

So I did. I sat down at my usual desk and wrote, "Dear Ms. Hanson—I am sorry that I was snooping around your classroom. I am also sorry that I hid under your desk. And I am very, very sorry that my face got in the way of your pointy shoe. Love, Keena Ford." I drew a sad face next to my name so she would know I was very sorry. Then I gave the letter to Mr. Lemon.

He said, "I suppose now you must write an apology to Ms. Campbell for not following directions."

My eyes got wet again. "Ms. Campbell hates me now," I said. "I hurt her feelings."

Mr. Lemon asked me what I was talking about. I told him how Eric said that

I had wished I could be in Ms. Hanson's class. "I said it," I told Mr. Lemon, "but that's not what I meant! I meant I just wanted to be in their class for the pudding pie." I told Mr. Lemon that I loved my class. And I didn't mean to make my teacher sad.

"Well, Miss Ford," said Mr. Lemon, "I suppose you can explain yourself to Ms. Campbell in your letter."

This is what I wrote: "Dear Ms. Campbell—I am sorry that I broke the rules by sneaking into Ms. Hanson's room and hiding under her desk. I am also very, very sorry to have hurt your feelings. I do not think Ms. Hanson's class is more fun than our class. I think you are the very best teacher in the whole world. I love you very much. I hope you forgive me. Love, Keena Ford." Next to my name I drew a REALLY sad face with two tears coming out of the eyes. Then I drew a broken heart.

I showed my note to Mr. Lemon. Then I started to talk. Sometimes when I have to go to Mr. Lemon's class, all my thoughts come out. I told him that Linny Berry and I were going to be friends again. I told him about how Eric had lied to me about Ms. Hanson's class. I said that I didn't understand why Eric would make up all of those stories.

Mr. Lemon said, "Well, Miss Ford, has anyone ever gotten to do something that you wanted to do but couldn't?"

I said yes. I said everyone got to go to Linny's birthday party but me.

"And how did that make you feel?" Mr. Lemon asked.

"Jealous," I told him.

"So how do you think Eric feels about your very exciting class and your new friendship with Linny Berry?"

I only had to think for about three seconds. "Jealous," I said again.

Then I asked Mr. Lemon if I could write one more note.

"Dear Eric," I wrote. "I am sorry if I

made you feel jealous about my teacher. I am also very sorry if I made you feel jealous of Linny Berry. You are still my very best friend. Love, Keena Ford." Next to my name I drew a boy and a girl smiling. I wrote "E" on the boy's shirt and "K" on the girl's shirt. Then I wrote "Best Friends."

I showed my letter to Mr. Lemon. He said that I could go back to class. I gave my letters to Ms. Hanson and Ms. Campbell. Then I tried to be very quiet for the rest of the day.

When the bell rang I tried to get out of the classroom as fast as I could. But I ran right into Ms. Hanson in the hallway. She looked down at me. She looked very, very serious. "Keena," she said, "you should not have gone in my classroom and hidden under the desk. But thank you for the apology. I think you have learned your lesson." Then she smiled! I nodded my head. "Yes, ma'am," I said. "It will never happen again."

Then I heard Ms. Campbell calling me from the classroom. "Keena, please come back here for a moment," she said.

I walked back into the classroom.

"I just wanted to give you this," Ms. Campbell said. She handed me a piece of paper that was folded in half. "Thank you," I whispered. I could tell it was a letter. And I knew what it said. It said that Ms. Campbell tried to love me, but she just couldn't because I had done two very bad things. I had pretended it was my birthday when it really wasn't, and I had said I wanted to be in Ms. Hanson's class. I put the letter in my backpack. I decided to wait until I got home to read it, because I didn't want Ms. Campbell to see me cry again.

Eric and this fifth grader named Lamont were waiting for me by the front door of the school. We are always supposed to walk home together. I was going to tell Eric that I was sorry, but

I just handed him his note instead. He didn't open it. We didn't talk the whole way home. Even though it was only two blocks, it felt just like the time when we didn't speak for three whole days.

As soon as I got home I went to my room. I got Ms. Campbell's letter out of my backpack and I started to read.

"Dear Keena," it said. "I forgive you. It is always good to say you're sorry when you make a mistake. Please remember the rules next time! I know you will try. Love, Ms. Campbell." And next to her name she drew a smiley face.

A smiley face meant that Ms. Campbell didn't hate me after all! Right then I made a plan. The next time Ms. Campbell said, "Good morning, Keena!" I wasn't just going to say good morning. I was going to give her a GREAT BIG HUG.

8:00 P.M

Eric came by after dinner. He said, "Thanks for the note." Then he said, "Sorry I lied about my classroom."

"It's okay," I told him.

Then Eric said that maybe we should fix up the Homework Hut after all. Even if we didn't have the same homework, we both still needed a quiet place to work. I

said I thought that was a smart idea.

I ran to my room and got my art box. Eric and I went onto the balcony and uncovered the Homework Hut. First we repainted the letters so that it said "Homework Hut" again. We blew on the letters to help them dry, until we got kind of dizzy. Before we put the cover back on the Homework Hut, we sat inside it, just to test it out.

Then I said maybe we should make some rules for the Homework Hut. "The first rule in the Homework Hut," I said, "is that you CAN chew gum."

"And the second rule," said Eric, "is that you can write in pen."

SATURDAY, SEPTEMBER 4
11:30 A.M.

It is Saturday. Brian is in DC practicing for basketball tryouts already, and I am at Dad's house. This morning when Dad picked me up, he asked Mom, "How was Keena's first week of second grade?" My heart started to beat fast while I waited for Mom to answer. She put her arm around me and gave me a squeeze. "I think Keena has already learned quite a lot in second grade," Mom said. She smiled at Dad and then at me. "I'll let her tell you all about it." I smiled back at Mom, and she gave me a big hug. "Have a good weekend, Valentine," she said.

Dad and I walked outside to his car. "I can't wait to hear all about second grade," he said. I told him we should probably go out for coffee. "It's going to be a LONG story," I said.